Hope, Time,
and Other Things
That Are Hard to Measure

A Tale by Maria Glymph

A Modern Odyssey Book

ISBN: 979-8-9900395-6-8

Modern Odyssey Books
Maria Glymph, Publisher
www.modernodysseybooks.com

Cover Photo Credit: The cover photo is credited to Canva and used with permission via our Pro subscription. As you can see it was perfect in telling Caleb's story. We gratefully acknowledge its use.

for Tom

Jake looked out of the window as the rain slowly fell. The panes cried for Christmas to remain, but the snow had long melted away and the once glorious pine lay on the curb waiting.

Jake sighed. "Why does it have to end if it was only the beginning?" he said out loud. He moved closer to the glass, peering outside, and saw the tree through his memory – colored lights, silver tinsel, and the big gold star that he made in Miss Bishop's class. He smiled thinking about all the ornaments: the nutcracker his father brought back from Germany, the hand-painted cardinal his grandmother gave him last year, the drummer boy he… *Oh forget it!* he thought.

"I don't understand why Mom says that for everything there is a season. Why can't we have Christmas winter, Christmas spring, Christmas summer, and Christmas fall? I mean who *wouldn't* want that?!" He spoke to no one in particular; he was alone in his bedroom.

BEEP. BEEP. BEEP. Jake could hear a truck coming down the street. He shouted to his mom, "I think the truck is here for the tree."

Jake's mother responded in a happy tone, "Goodbye beautiful tree!"

As Jake turned toward the sound of his mother's voice, his eyes fell upon the highest bookshelf.

"Oh no!"

Jake looked up and down, left and right. He turned round and looked on the floor, back to the shelves, around all the other books. He spun himself in circles.

"Where is he?!"

Jake ran down the hall to find his mother.

"Mom! Mom! He's gone! We've got to stop the truck."

"Jake, calm down. What are you talking about?"

"It's Caleb, he's still on the tree."

"Who's Caleb?"

"The camel. He's the camel ornament on the tree."

"Honey, we don't have a camel ornament."

BEEP. BEEP. BEEP. The truck was in front of the house.

"Yes, we do, I put him on the tree myself. He's from David."

Jake was desperate.

"David? Who's David? Jake calm down. I put all the ornaments away. Not one of them was missing."

BEEP. BEEP. BEEP.

Alarmed, Jake ran to the living room window. The truck had stopped. Two men in green uniforms were hoisting the tree into the hopper. The rain weeping down the windows blurred the image of the tree and made the knotted tinsel that remained sparkle like ice crystals.

Jake lowered his head and tears burned in the corner of his eyes. Caleb was gone forever.

As the men in green uniforms tossed the tree into the truck, Caleb dislodged from the low branch where he had been resting. He fell onto the street with a THUD, and with one swift gesture, the rain swept him into the opening of the storm drain.

"Yikes!" Caleb screamed. "What's happening?"

Caleb slipped and slithered as if he was on a long water slide. It was as black as a raven, and he traveled for what he knew was miles and miles – well, he didn't really know how far but he could accurately guess that it was a long distance. Water rushed around him, and he had a hard time keeping his head above his hump. He moved his legs back and forth as if he was swimming. With a sudden and urgent push from the water, Caleb was spat out into what seemed to be a placid pool only to be carried off once again by the galloping current. Caleb started to feel dizzy.

In the distance, he could see a light. It began to get brighter and brighter and bigger and bigger. And then...

When Caleb awoke, he was lying face down in the sand. The sun blazed. He opened his eyes, but it took a few minutes to adjust to the light. He spat out the grit in his mouth and shook his head back and forth to get it out of his nose. *Ow!* His head hurt from all the knocking about.

"What happened?"

He still felt a bit dizzy as he stood up.

"Mmm, that sure feels good." Caleb loved the sun. He knew it would warm him up and dry his coat. He looked around. He was on a beach that stretched as far as he could see in both directions. Trees the size of – well, he didn't know what size they were exactly but huge described them accurately. They were big, white, and lifeless, and they were lying on their sides. Several were in a tangle. Water pooled in a number of places in the sand. The ocean was flat all the way to its edge.

"Where am I?"

Caleb looked around but couldn't see anyone. Not a single soul. The beach was deserted.

"Where *is* everybody?"

Caleb felt hot and thirsty. He was also a bit bewildered – he knew he had just come through some long passage on a bumpy ride with lots of water, but he couldn't recall where he had come from and who he had been with. It was on the edge of his mind but too far out of reach.

His hump drooped. He walked to the water's edge and began to drink as the waves gently splashed against his legs. He drank and drank and drank and drank and drank and drank and drank.

Satisfied, he smacked his lips with his long tongue and said, "Yeah, that's enough for now."

Caleb looked around again, following the line

of the horizon with his gaze. Nothing. *Where was he*, he wondered. Suddenly, the gentle lapping rapidly grew into big waves splashing, and Caleb started to sink into the... "Quicksand!"

He panicked just as a log the size of – well, he didn't know what size it was. Anyway, a log came rushing at him with a shove from the waves. All he could do was grasp and hug the tree trunk as the tide pulled him out to sea with its white knuckled hands.

Caleb clutched the log, his legs wrapped around the circumference so that nothing or no one could possibly pry him off until he was back on land. The only problem was that he couldn't see any dry land. He had been tugged out to what seemed like the center of the world. It was an endless expanse of water. And it roared. It frightened him a little. Okay, it frightened him a lot.

Caleb began to hum – a quiet, murmuring tune that soothed him whenever he was scared or nervous. *Hmm hmm hmm. Hmm hmm hmm hmm hmm.* In the middle of a vast, unknown body of water, Caleb gripped the wood, his muscles stiffened, and the log swayed. *Hmm hmm hmm.*

There wasn't anything he could do but hold onto the log. He didn't know what was in the water beneath him, and he wouldn't peer over the side of the log for fear that he would fall off. So, he held on. He tried to stay alert, but the sun caressed him. He dozed in and out of sleep.

He dreamt of a boy, though he couldn't see him clearly. The boy brushed his coat and smoothed it out. The boy spoke softly and said, "Don't worry, I have plans for you." He kept repeating this, and the boy also said, "I'm doing this to give you hope and a future." In his dream, Caleb tried to ask, "What plans? What plans?" And then he woke with a start. *What*, he wondered, *is my future?*

When he wasn't sleeping, Caleb thought. And thought. And thought. He tried to recall where he had come from. He had a vague notion of a friend, *perhaps the boy?* but he couldn't pull more than that from his memory. His mind buzzed like a beehive. *What are the odds? A camel on a log in the middle of an ocean going somewhere toward the edge of the world. But why? Is the future on the other side of the world?*

Caleb felt that deep within he already knew the answer, but what was in his heart wouldn't come to his head. It frustrated him, but at the same time and in some unexplainable way, it comforted him, and so he settled into the days knowing that the purpose of this journey would reveal itself. It was his future.

Days passed.

Caleb didn't mind the days so much. He watched the clouds gather and take shape, and in them he saw pirates and kings and crocodiles and foxes. He was glad for the company. Vessels passed on the horizon, too far away for contact, but they were a comfort because the sight of them made Caleb feel less alone.

The birds did too. So many different kinds. Some plunged into the water. Some landed on the surface and sat on top to rest. Sometimes they squawked at each other or complained or cackled. Caleb found them funny. He also spied orcas, sharks, and dolphins. Some came close enough to displace the water around him, but mostly he viewed them in the distance. The wind either howled or whispered, and somewhere in its throat Caleb heard words of solace – *do not be dismayed; do not be discouraged; do not lose heart*; and on and on.

The nights were challenging and scary. He hummed a lot. Everything was dark. It was dark above, and it was dark below. Caleb feared what he could not see and what he didn't understand. The ocean was not familiar to a camel. He fathomed endless grains of sand but was perplexed by drops of water – at least this many, and he had no idea how many drops the ocean contained. He was not good at measurements – time, distance, length, width, weight – but he knew magnitude, and that's why he felt that his journey was important and significant. Something about the boy in his dream stirred within, and he vowed that he would face whatever came with courage and patience.

When the dark curtain of the night dropped, stars slowly appeared. Then more. Then even more. And then the dome above his head was flooded with light. Whenever he saw a shooting star, Caleb wondered if it was moving forward or backward in time. The night sky was a chronicle of the past, and it also contained the future. His future.

The wind blew cold and bellowed, and yet it continued to encourage – *be strong and brave; hope for what you do not see; wait for it with patience.*

Back and forth went the days and nights.

One clear day, Caleb bobbed along relishing the way the sun felt on his coat. He was trying to recall what he had been doing before he was thrust into the water chute.

Suddenly a giant fish jumped out of the dark abyss and soared toward heaven cutting the sky with a long spear extending from its nose.

"Whoa-oh-oh-oh-oh." Caleb felt like clapping, but he didn't want to risk letting go of the log.

With a thunderous SPLASH, the marlin descended back into the deep.

It was quiet for some time. The wind blew low and gentle, taking a break from its wave making. The sun continued to radiate, and Caleb felt relaxed. Like searchlights, his eyes crisscrossed the horizon looking for… for what he wasn't quite sure, but he was hoping to see something. *Another marlin would be cool,* he thought.

Some black specks on the horizon became thicker and then collectively they came toward him in a formation. As the dots took shape, they became birds, and as they became birds, they swooped around him.

"Ahoy down there!"

Caleb wanted to wave but didn't want to chance losing his grip. "Hey up there," he said. He lifted his head to the sky so the sound of his voice could rise to greet them.

"You okay? Know where you're headed?"

"I'm alright." Said Caleb. "Not sure where I'm going." He made a gesture to indicate being confined to the log as if to say "Can't you tell?" but instead said "Where you headed?"

"We're going home, just like you," they spoke as one voice, one with a sing-song quality to it. In unison, they dropped and tumbled and spun and rolled and then jetted upward and zigzagged downward. Caleb's eyes followed their aerobatic maneuvers. *How wonderful to be a bird*, he thought.

"It is indeed, Caleb," they said.

"Wait, how did you know what I was thinking? How do you know my name? And what do you mean going home just like me?" Caleb couldn't ask the questions fast enough.

And then, as quickly as they had come, they were gone. And once again, he was alone.

After some time, the sky rearranged the sun into a new position and scattered billowing clouds. Caleb entertained himself by following the crest of a wave as it rolled along the ocean. When he lost sight of one, he'd find another. He sighed and shifted his position just so, and with this small, seemingly insignificant movement, the log flipped over.

Instinctively, he squeezed his eyes shut, his long lashes locking together, and pushed his face against the wood. Caleb was now on the underside of the log. And then he heard a voice – actually, it was several voices.

"Yo!"

"Sup man?"

Caleb jerked his eyes open. What did he see? A flotilla of swordfish, just a short distance away, were dueling in pairs as if they were training for the Olympics. They laughed as they called out to him. Further away in another direction, a smack of jellyfish looked like bells with streamers, their long tentacles dancing to some strange choreography. An army of herring swam past playing capture-the-flag with two pieces of floating seaweed, and a handful of sharks occupied themselves with a game of tag, darting around Caleb and everyone else. It was a riot of activity.

Holy cow!

The water was clear, and he could see for a long distance. The groups of sea creatures were all around him. Just beyond, a gloomy canyon betrayed the menacing mystery of the deep. Caleb shuddered.

Where did they all come from? I thought I was alone out here.

"You're not alone." Spoke a soothing voice.

Caleb turned to see a sizable – just how big he

couldn't say, but it was substantial – octopus with sleepy eyes and a Cheshire grin.

"You're never alone, Caleb."

The only thing Caleb could do was blink. He wanted to say something, to ask a question, or maybe ask lots of questions, but he was transfixed. Every muscle in his body was stiff, and yet his mind hurried. Silently he wondered:

Who are you?

What do you mean?

Who's always with me?

And how do you know my name?

What's happening down here?

An Octopus with teeth?

And on and on.

"You're on your way home, Caleb. When you flip back over and continue your odyssey, look up to the heavens and count the stars. Then close your eyes for sleep. Doves will come to you in your dreams, and they will fly high above and back and forth. When one brings you a twig, you will have arrived at the path home." As he spoke, his arms writhed and twisted, and when he finished, his limbs configured themselves into the shape of a rocket and he darted away. The movement of the water flipped Caleb back up to the ocean's surface.

That's crazy. Is that some kind of riddle? What was that about?

Caleb floated along thinking about the toothy octopus. He dozed off and on under the warm gaze of the sun. The ocean undulated, and occasionally a splash of water would tickle one of Caleb's legs or his side. He thought about everything he had heard, he thought about where he was going – he still wasn't sure – and where he had come from – he wasn't sure about that either. At the horizon of his mind, he thought about the boy. He recognized a feeling of safety and comfort and hope, and these thoughts steadied him as the sea pitched and rolled him and the log toward the edge of the earth. But still, he hummed.

The sun decided to hide. The vault of heaven changed colors. Ancient time began to sparkle in the sky. Caleb remembered what the octopus said about counting the stars, so he did, and before long he fell into a deep slumber.

In a twinkling, the ocean began to boil, and the water gurgled in big gulps. A towering vortex formed, and its spiraling force pulled everything toward its dark center. Caleb began to spin helplessly. Waves crashed violently around the edges of the whirlpool. And just as he was being sucked into the middle, a dove visited him.

Caleb woke with a start. His nose was clogged, and a sneeze was quickly surging. Instead of water, he was surrounded by a billion grains of sand – well, he couldn't say it was a billion exactly, but it was millions for sure.

He had made it to land. *Land!* He and the log lay on a beach.

Where he was, he did not know. The octopus's words echoed in his ears. *I'm going home,* he thought, and he turned the word *home* over in his mind, examining it to try to understand what exactly it meant: a place of belonging, a place of comfort, a place of love and warmth, a place where the boy was. *Home.* Caleb stood up and started walking toward the sun.

Time, for Caleb, had lost all meaning. He didn't know how long he had been on this journey, and he had absolutely no sense in which hour of the day he found himself. The position of the sun provided a vague notion of the daily cycle but otherwise he was as lost in time as he was on this trek.

He walked until he was tired, rested under the shade of an Acacia tree whenever he could find one, and then walked until he was tired again. He walked across places that were forgotten by the feet of people and animals. And he walked as if he knew the way home. He thought he heard music and singing, but decided it was fatigue. Sometimes, he'd hear a crystal-clear voice tell him not to be discouraged or afraid. He would look up and see a desert sparrow darting away. Another voice encouraged him to not grow weary and not be faint. Again, he looked up, but this time a lark flew past.

After what seemed like an eon – though he

didn't really know how long that was – he spied a group of four-legged creatures in the distance. His heart fluttered, and he started running toward what he knew was not a mirage.

As he got closer, he realized the animals he could see were camels. "Hallelujah!" Then he realized that they had two humps. *Wait, what?* Thought Caleb. *Why two humps? That's weird.*

Caleb approached the camels with tentative steps. They flattened their ears and shifted and opened their positions as a sign of welcome. Caleb lowered his head and glanced at each camel to make eye contact and discern each of their stances. He viewed them with curiosity – they were short and stocky and had two humps – and they peered at him with interest – he was taller and thinner and had only one hump. They were the same and yet different.

"Hey man, you okay?"

"Good heavens I'm glad to see you!" Caleb practically shouted with joy. He was relieved and happy. "Yes, I'm fine. I've traveled across the desert and haven't come across a single soul. Just a few desert birds. You're a sight for lonely eyes."

The camels were friendly and talkative. They told Caleb that they were part of a tribe camped nearby and pointed toward a cluster of tents. Caleb hadn't noticed the encampment or the people or the activity until that moment.

The tents were grouped casually. They had wide openings, and Caleb could see rugs spread across the tent floors. Cushions lined the perimeters. Men sat in small clusters smoking hookah pipes. Outside, two women cooked bread on an open griddle. Another stirred a cauldron of bubbling liquid. An assortment of people milked animals, prepared food, repaired tents, wove rugs, and mended clothing.

The camels had never seen one of their kind with only one hump. They came closer to Caleb and inspected his body.

"That's radical, man," said one.

"No, no, that's epic is what that is," said another.

"One is good, but two is better," said a third.

His playful smile revealed two oversized front teeth.

They gawked, and Caleb felt awkward. He avoided their eyes and just looked down at the sand. One of them, named Jamal, snorted softly, and shifted his weight from side to side maintaining an agnostic attitude. He kept his neck stiff and his head high. Caleb sensed disinterest or dislike, but he couldn't tell which, and he noted that Jamal buried his opinion in the wrinkle of his smile.

The camels told Caleb about their nomadic life in the desert with the Bedouins. They were good people, the camels said, hardworking and light-hearted, caring for the animals and showing them consideration. The Bedouins fed and dressed the camels and always encouraged them and thanked them for their work and contributions to tribal life. The camels praised the leader of the tribe who they called Old Man, and they said that the clan numbered to forty.

The camels told Caleb about how the days

darkened and were then governed by the moon and stars. They slumbered under the tent of the heavens while the men and women and children slept in their woolen tents. The camels also told Caleb about how the light changed when midnight crawled to dawn, how some days felt like living in a furnace, and how the desert took off its disguise to reveal frogs, snakes, lizards, birds, and so many other hidden creatures. They said that they often traveled at night because it was cooler, using the constellations to navigate. The camels went on and on. When they spoke of the sun, they referred to it as the Big Kahuna and spoke with reverence.

Then, it was Caleb's turn. The camels wanted to know all about him, and just as they began to ask Caleb where he had come from, the Old Man walked up with greetings.

"Peace be upon you. Welcome and may you find ease and comfort here with us." He wore loose clothes cinched at the waist and a cloth wrapped over his head. Other than his face and hands, he was completely sheltered from the sun.

"Thank you. Everyone's been so kind already. I'm just so glad to have found all of you." Caleb smiled. "I tired of being by myself on my travels."

"Tell us," said the Old Man.

So, Caleb told them everything – at least everything he could remember. He recounted his journey down the dark water slide, his encounter with quicksand and getting pulled out to sea, his time on the log in the middle of the ocean, and the harrowing experience of the whirlpool. He described the birds, the fish, and the octopus. He told of not knowing from where he came or exactly to where he was going, but that he had been guided by the wind, the birds, and others to keep going and not be afraid. And he told of his vague recollection of the boy. Caleb was open about being nervous and scared, and he said that he felt a strong sense of purpose, although mysterious, and that it gave him courage and comfort. The words tumbled out of his mouth and cast vivid images of his pilgrimage in the minds of the others.

The camels were enthralled with his description of the ocean, the fighting fish, and wise old octopus. "That's righteous!" The camels stared at him in wonder, some with their tongues hanging out of their mouths. It was all so foreign. The Old Man nodded.

They invited him to stay with them, but Caleb declined. Something inside him stirred with urgency, and he told them that he needed to continue his journey. They insisted. His voyage had been long and tiring, they said, he needed rest and nourishment so that his body and his mind would be prepared to cross the barren landscape that lay ahead. Their hospitality touched Caleb, and he was relieved to be around others after a long spell of loneliness. Caleb agreed to stay.

"According to an old custom," said the Old Man. "We host festivals based on the wandering stars. In three days, we will celebrate again."

"It's going to be great. We have races, we tell stories, we play music, and we eat and eat and eat," said one of the camels. Then he dragged his long tongue around his mouth and across his lips.

"That sounds cool. What kind of races?" asked Caleb.

"Camel races," said the Old Man. "You can participate."

Jamal shifted his weight.

"You can also tell your stories," the Old Man said. "We will eat and drink and be glad." And all the camels nodded their heads.

"Sounds fun," said Caleb. The burden of his odyssey fell from his shoulders, and his feet felt lighter. It had been a long trek – how long he didn't know exactly, but days had passed and then more days had passed.

"You'll stay with the other camels," said the Old Man. "Let us know what you may need. Ask and it will be given to you." He smiled and his eyes sparkled. He turned to leave and then turned back. "Do you know that in a race all the runners run, but only one gets the prize?" He paused. "Run in such a way as to get the prize."

He walked away.

Another riddle? Caleb couldn't be sure.

Caleb savored everyone's affability, but at the same time, he noted that Jamal kept his eyes hooded and his convictions hidden. Caleb overheard a couple of the camels tell Jamal not to judge for he too would be judged. Jamal just grunted. Caleb heard another call Jamal a nimrod. Caleb smiled to himself, but not because Jamal was being called names. Instead, Caleb grinned at the friendship, the kindness, the belonging. Even though the octopus told him that he's never alone, that's exactly how he had felt as he traveled.

The Bedouin camp was lively, and Caleb liked hearing the voices and the laughter and the hubbub. And as for Jamal? Caleb could see that Jamal's discomfort was with what he didn't understand – a single hump. Caleb was unfamiliar, and it would take Jamal some time to overcome his unease.

Caleb and his new friends spent the next two days fooling around, climbing, racing, and making tracks across the dunes. They laughed a lot and fell into amiable teasing about the differences between camels with one hump and those with two. Caleb couldn't recall a time when he had so much fun (though it reminded him of what he saw in the ocean), and that is exactly what it was – pure fun and games and joy.

Caleb and the camels liked the dunes and the way they shifted and changed shape, and they liked the way the wind created designs with the sand. Racing up and down and over them was *a blast!*

They had set up several contests to see who could sprint the fastest over a particular dune, and because each dune was different, each race was unique. Caleb had won the first one and pranced around swishing his tail. This caused Jamal to grunt and everyone else to sigh. The second competition was about to begin.

"And let us run with perseverance the race marked out for us," said one camel.

"That's fancy for run like wind," said another.

They all laughed.

A gentle breeze kept the camels cool all morning, but suddenly the wind became muscular and began to lift the grains of sand into the air. Instinctively, Caleb and his friends shut their nostrils. The swift wind whirled and agitated the sand. Twisters rose from the ground and clustered together making visibility impossible. It became dark and Caleb couldn't see beyond a few feet. He stopped. He turned round and round but couldn't see anything or anyone. He walked slowly, looking left and right for one of the other camels. The wind howled around him. He lowered his eyelids so that only a slant of light would guide his way. He turned round. He turned left. He turned right. He stopped. *I'll just stay here until this is over*, he thought. He closed his eyes completely and hunkered down.

After a while – Caleb didn't know how much time had passed – the furious wind subsided, and he opened his eyes. Nothing was familiar. He looked around but didn't see any of the other camels, and the storm had changed the landscape so much so that he didn't recognize anything in any direction. He decided to walk toward some canyons in the distance in case he needed to take cover.

No sooner had he started walking than the wind dusted up once more, the sky quickly darkened, and a thunderstorm struck. Lightning rippled across the horizon and flashes of electric current zigzagged to the ground. Caleb picked up speed. Drops of water soon transformed into compact peas of ice and began to pelt Caleb.

Oh no! Hail!

Caleb began to run. His eyes scanned the canyons for a place to shelter. He spied a spot about halfway up a jagged trail. Caleb moved faster as the sky spit hail without aim. Frozen rain pelted his head and back. He kept running.

Caleb climbed toward what looked like a cave a few hundred feet up –well, he didn't know it was a few hundred feet, he wasn't good at distance – and he decided to head there, dodging hailstones, keeping steady footing on the rocky path. He was almost to the entrance when a big – how big he didn't know because he didn't see it – ball of ice hit him in the back between his shoulder blades. *Ouch! Youwza! That hurt!* It was like hitting the funny bone – although there was nothing funny about it. He felt a sharp pain that grew and radiated through his whole body.

Caleb jerked and lost his footing, and he fell onto his front knees. His face barely missed a sharp rock. The hail continued to rain down on him, but he couldn't get up. Caleb's right ankle throbbed. He raised his head in hopes of hearing the encouraging voices to which he had become accustomed, and before he knew what was happening, four men were helping him up and guiding him to the cave.

Greetings, grace and peace to you."

Caleb's eyes adjusted quickly, and he saw four men. They sat down around an unlit fire pit. They were skinny as saints and dressed in long wool coats that had patches and tears and looked like they had been washed in mud.

"Thanks, you too," Caleb said. He looked around. "Thank you for helping me. Mind if I wait here until the storm passes?"

"You're not going to go too far on that ankle," said one of the men. "You'll need to wait until you're healed. That'll be longer than waiting for the storm to pass."

"You're welcome to stay here," said another.

The man first to speak approached Caleb and began to touch his right ankle.

"Easy does it," said Caleb. He winced.

"You likely just twisted it on a rock. A light sprain at most. Nothing to worry about. I know exactly what you need." The man rose and dashed outside. He came back a few minutes later with two handfuls of hail which he packed together and applied to Caleb's ankle. "It'll be fine."

Once again, Caleb found himself in benevolent company. He discovered that the men were hermits who had found sanctuary in the cave. For some reason they were named after the four directions – East, West, North, and South. Caleb thought it odd but didn't have time to ask how they got their names.

Because Caleb wore an aura of curiosity, the hermits fed it with their biographies and stories. They met at a desert watering hole. Each had been living in isolation, scattered in the four directions, dedicating themselves fully to prayer.

After meeting, they decided to live communally yet still allowing for solitude. They envisioned a simpler life, sharing their energies and resources, creating time for contemplation as well as fellowship. They had been together for many years. North was the man who had tended to his ankle.

East pulled a harmonica from his pocket.

"We love to sing and tell stories," he said.

West beamed a smile, and South nodded. East brought the harmonica to his lips and began to blow a tune. North led the lyrics with "Though like the wanderer, the sun gone down…" and the others joined. Caleb settled into a comfortable position and then caught on to the chorus and sang along, "Nearer, my God, to Thee."

Time passed, though Caleb couldn't say exactly how much time had gone by. They sang and talked and talked and sang. Caleb thought about his camel friends and wondered if they were okay and if they would be worrying about him. He didn't know if he would ever see them again. Deep inside, he doubted it, and deep inside, he knew he was right. He told the hermits about the camels and the tribe. West encouraged Caleb to cherish the memories of their brief time together. It had been a gift of true friendship, he said. Caleb agreed, and that included Jamal, who he thought might also be feeling his absence. Caleb smiled.

Caleb marveled that one friendly encounter led to the next, particularly since he was alone for so long until he met the camels. The octopus did say that he was never alone, and perhaps the octopus was right. It might just be a matter of recognizing who and what is around you, and with you. Caleb continued his attempt at deciphering the meaning of the cephalopod's words. He felt sure it was a riddle.

The singing continued until it was time for more storytelling. The hermits knew many tales but wanted to hear from Caleb first. So once again he recounted his journey down the water chute, across the ocean, and through the desert. He described the days and nights, the fish and the birds, and the sandstorm and the hailstorm. He spoke of loneliness and solitude, and he told of the encouraging and comforting voices of the wind and the birds. Caleb spoke of the unknown destination of his journey, and he shared that he knew he was on his way to do something important. He knew because somewhere at the edge of his mind was a boy who cared for him, a boy who had plans for him.

The hermits listened intently. The octopus sounded magnificent, and all four glimpsed his big smile in their minds as Caleb shared his saga. They found the quicksand puzzling and asked questions about how it felt and if it was frightening. Camels with two humps were a site none of them had seen and one they couldn't imagine. Caleb realized he had seen and experienced a great deal – a thought that hadn't occurred to him until this moment.

The hermits, in turn, began to tell their stories. Caleb found that they wove the most amazing narratives, and some were beyond belief. From North came a story about a husband and wife who were evicted from their land because they ate apples. Evidently their landlord, though a kindhearted man, explicitly stated some restrictions to living on the property, and the couple showed poor judgement by not abiding by them. His punishment was swift and had long-lasting consequences for the generations that came after. *Those must have been some tasty apples*, thought Caleb.

South spun a story about a village that grew bigger and bigger and bigger because so many people came to live there. But there was a problem: they couldn't understand each other when they spoke. South switched between various languages – all foreign to Caleb – and used his hands to gesture. The others were captivated, but the story didn't really make sense to Caleb. *Perhaps South might be making his point*, thought Caleb.

West, it turned out, was as skillful as a magician when he told stories, and before long, he conjured up a ladder as wide as a roadway that transported people up to and down from the sky.

They wore flowing robes and were careful not to trip as they ascended and descended. They passed each other, smiled, and went on their way. West didn't say where they were coming from or where they were going. In no time, the ladder turned into a rushing river, its banks teeming with papyrus reeds, grasses, and rushes. An elegant princess, adorned with great beauty, heard a cry, and spotted a basket floating in the rushing water. As it knocked against the shore, she discovered a baby boy and quickly scooped him up. Once she lifted him out of the vessel, the river transformed into a sea, and a whale breached the surface, opened its mouth wide, swallowed a man, and then slowly slid back into the water.

"But," West paused.

Caleb and the others leaned forward, waiting.

"The whale did not like the taste of the man, and with one powerful push, it spit him out and then burped."

Ew! Thought Caleb. He shook his head. "Whale saliva, how gross!" he said.

West continued: No sooner had the man landed in the water, than the sea parted, and a parade of people walked through it crossing from one shore to the next.

"You're the best," said South. He clapped.

North and East applauded as well. Caleb hooted. He had never heard such incredible tales. The hermits were master storytellers. Caleb liked these otherworldly men who seemed to know … what, he wasn't sure, but he knew that they held uncommon wisdom. They laughed with their eyes and their smiles, radiating an aura of mystery. As the light left the cave, they lit a fire and their shadows danced on the walls to the sound of their voices.

Two days later, Caleb rose early. East, West, North, and South had been up with dawn. They had gone out to forage and returned with twigs and wood and berries and herbs. Caleb thanked them for their hospitality and assured them that he would keep them in his thoughts always and that he would never forget their stories. They encouraged him to retell them, and he promised he would. He left to resume his quest. A rainbow stretched across the horizon in front of him. A moody, grey sky was at his back.

En route to wherever he was headed, Caleb felt his path had been made straighter, and he soon encountered a caravan. It was long – how long, he couldn't say for sure, but it stretched from the horizon and there were hundreds – well he couldn't say for sure that there were hundreds, but it certainly looked like hundreds – of camels and people and cargo. They were the floating citizenry of a procession heading from one horizon to the other. It was said, by whom Caleb couldn't quite remember, that camels were the ships of the desert, and this was proof, as the parcels were piled high, and the beasts were loaded down.

For obvious reasons, they couldn't stop to

greet him, so Caleb sidled up to a man with an open and expressive face. He said he was on the way to his father's hometown to participate in a census. Several of the men were traders expanding commercial ties for their goods and those of other merchants. The caravan carried colorful carpets, reams of cloth, spices, tea, porcelain, and exotic merchandise from far off lands. Further ahead, he met a few explorers who spoke vaguely about where they were headed, and then Caleb spoke to a couple of the camels who were part of a large herd being transported to new land. Finally, Caleb trotted ahead and met a family with two small children who welcomed him and said that they were almost at their next destination, a caravanserai only a few miles ahead. They would rest for the night, there would be food and drink, and they would exchange some of their goods. The man and his wife invited Caleb to come along and rest at the inn.

The caravanserai rose from the sand like a mirage. It was immense. The outer walls housed rooms which quartered travelers or stored goods. The vast inner courtyard vibrated with the babble of merchants and sellers and dealers. Items were weighed on oversized brass scales. Baskets were passed around. Men smoked tall water pipes. Dogs laid around barking half-heartedly in the heat. A small stage was wedged into one corner, with five short rows of seats that were all full of bobbing heads. Puppets played out a story about a giant and a boy with a sling shot.

Caleb stood with his mouth agape as he drank in the scene.

Five female camels talked and swayed their hips. They stood next to several towering piles of carpets and periodically one of their hips would gently nudge the stacks. These ladies tittered as they glanced about under their long eyelashes. Four of them wore colorful tassels and gold chains, and their humps were covered in sumptuous fabric with shinning threads. One was different, and Caleb thought she was the real beauty. She was unadorned and yet she emanated a gentle, quiet spirit and a loving inner soul. *You have to look past shiny objects to find the real treasure,* thought Caleb.

"Psst." The voice penetrated Caleb's attention. "Hey you, come over here."

Caleb looked around and saw a vulture sitting on the top of a pole.

"Yeah, I'm talking to you. Come over here."

Caleb hesitantly started toward the raptor when a tall, plump man wearing brilliant-colored slippers, a wide-brimmed straw hat, and a white djellaba lumbered toward him with his head down. The man stopped and looked up and into Caleb's eyes. He said, "I was eyes to the blind and feet to the injured, I fathered the needy and protected the stranger, I broke the fangs of the evil ones and snatched the victims from their teeth."

"Move along buddy," said the vulture.

"What's he talking about?" asked Caleb.

"The price of wisdom is beyond rubies," said the man as he shuffled away.

Caleb began to hum.

"Never mind him. He's mad." The vulture shot a glance at the man as he walked away. "Hey, listen, I need your help. Come over here."

"What kind of help?"

"Come over here. What are you waiting for? Kingdom come?"

Caleb approached slowly.

"I want you to walk around this place and take a look at who is selling what, and then I want you to come back and tell me what you saw."

"Why?"

"What's with all the questions?"

"Why don't you do it? You've got wings. You can fly around and see for yourself." Caleb was a bit annoyed, but also intrigued by this audacious bird.

"Because. I want you to do it. These guys have lots of stuff," he swept the perimeter with his beak. "Too much. They don't need it all. I work with some folks – they're not in here, they're out there, and he pointed over his shoulder with his wing. They've asked me to locate a few items, so to speak, and you can help me find out who has what I'm looking for."

"Are you talking about stealing?" Caleb was incredulous. "You can't just take other people's stuff." He hummed louder.

"Why not?"

"Because. It's wrong. And it's a crime. Because they've worked hard for it."

"Don't be naïve kid. And stop making that noise."

They went back and forth and back and forth

as the vulture tried to convince Caleb to support his nefarious efforts.

"You know that money is the root of all evil," said Caleb.

"Let me guess." The vulture rolled his eyes with exaggeration. "Now you're going to tell me that no one can serve two masters." He looked up at the sky. "I know. I know. I've heard it all before."

Caleb shook his head indicating disapproval.

"You know if you do this for me, my friends will respect you."

Caleb shook his head.

"Come on now, rules, like laws, are meant to be broken. Don't be such a literalist."

Caleb shook his head.

"We could become partners. My brains, your muscles."

Caleb shook his head.

"Just this once?"

Caleb wasn't naïve. He knew to be careful with characters like this, who tried to manipulate and exploit. Caleb was steadfast and would not be tempted no matter what the vulture dangled in front of him as an enticement.

"You disappoint me," said the vulture.

Caleb hated hearing those words even if they came from a hoodlum. Caleb liked helping people. No matter the task, he always offered support. But this, this was not something he would do.

"I thought you might be the one," said the big, black bird. "I'll just have to find someone else." And with that, he turned and flew up to the roof and began walking the length of it.

Caleb was relieved to be free of his company. The day had worn him out, and so had the vulture. He needed some sleep. He found an empty spot along perimeter in front of an empty storage room, sat down to rest, and fell into a deep slumber. He dreamed of the stories that the hermits had told, and of the octopus with teeth. He dreamed of the Old Man, and of the stars in the night sky. He dreamed of the gangster bird, then of a man gesticulating and pointing at Caleb. *Who was that?* Caleb stirred.

It wasn't a dream. A portly man stood above him talking to several other men who had gathered around. They were all dressed like the Old Man. The overweight one said, "Gather round. This is a very unique offering, an opportunity that doesn't surface very often. Here is a young, strong camel, look at him." He pointed to Caleb. "He's ready to work hard, loves to work hard." The man narrowed his eyes. "He's ready to work for you."

"How much?" said one man.

"Make him stand," said another.

Caleb came to his senses and realized that the portly man was trying to sell him. *Sell me!*

Caleb stood and felt the noose the portly man had hung around his neck while he was sleeping. The other end of the rope lay on the ground. Caleb looked around. The vulture sat high up on the pole laughing. The bazaar was thronged with people and wares. Caleb started to push through the crowd and trot through the maze of the market. At some point, the noose came undone and slipped away. He knocked over several baskets and carts and almost tumbled over some children under foot. The only thing Caleb could hear was the noise of tongues. The overweight man had started to chase him, but Caleb was too fast and the man too slow. Caleb picked up speed, navigated the labyrinth, headed for the gateway, and escaped into the desert.

Once again, he was alone. Once again, he was in the desert. Once again, he wasn't sure where he was headed. But once again, he heard the comforting voices – *do not let your hope tarnish; do not be dismayed; do not be discouraged; do not lose heart;* and on and on.

He kept running. He never looked back.

By and by, a broad Acacia tree appeared in the distance, and Caleb decided to stop and catch his breath underneath it. He was tired and began to mutter to himself. *When is the future going to get here? Who is the boy? How long do I need to be patient? Am I going in the right direction?*

"You are."

Caleb looked around but didn't see anyone.

"Who said that?"

"I did."

Caleb looked around again but didn't see anything or anyone.

"I'm up here."

Caleb raised his eyes to the branches of the

Acacia tree and discovered a lark peering down at him. It began to sing a beautiful song and turned its head up toward the sky. When it finished, the lark looked back down at Caleb.

"Beautiful. What were you singing about?"

"A shepherd. One who lovingly tends his flock. You'll meet him soon, Caleb."

"Wait, how do you know my name?"

"The shepherd told me. He said you would be coming this way." And then, she flew away.

"How is it that this keeps happening?" Caleb said to the wind, but he didn't receive a reply. He watched the path of the lark's flight and then he noticed a rider. Instinctively Caleb stood up and started running toward what looked like a man on a camel.

"Hey, wait! Wait up. Are you the shepherd?"

The man couldn't hear Caleb. He and his camel were traveling at a quick pace. Caleb increased his speed to gain ground on them. He could hear the lark's song in his mind. He was determined, pushing himself to go faster.

The man on the camel turned into two men on two camels, and finally they stopped. Their pause gave Caleb the break he needed, and he reached them just in time to say hello and collapse onto his front legs.

"Easy does it friend," said one.

"What's the hurry?" asked the other.

Caleb panted for a few minutes before he was able to utter a sound. And finally, he blurted out, "I'm lost!"

"Lost? Where are you headed?"

Caleb thought for a moment, then said, "I'm not sure. Are you shepherds?"

They noticed the bewildered look on Caleb's face, and one of them asked him his name.

"I'm Caleb."

"I'm Caspar," said the taller of the two men.

"And I'm Mel," said the other. "You're welcome to ride with us. We're not shepherds. Our path is along with the stars, and we're following a big one now."

"Come along," said Caspar. "We'll go slow

until you get your energy back."

The moon made itself visible and the light of the day faded. A campfire danced in the distance ahead of the travelers. When they reached it, a man was unloading heavy packs from a horse. He greeted them.

"What's the problem friend?" asked Caspar.

"The load is heavy, and the horse is weak from the trek across the sand."

The horse's shoulder and back muscles bulged, it shifted its weight back and forth, and it breathed deeply.

"Mind if we rest here in front of your fire?" asked Caspar.

"What's mine is yours," said the man.

"What's your name?" asked Mel.

"They call me Zar."

Introductions circled the campfire as everyone settled down close to the flame to ward off the chill spread by the sunset.

Caleb sympathized with the horse. He didn't know the content of the load but knew that he could carry it.

"Where are you headed?" asked Caleb.

"I follow the stars," said Zar.

"The one in the east?" asked Caspar.

"Yes. And you?"

"We, too, are guided by the path of that star. Perhaps we can ride together."

"My friends, that would be wonderful, but you may not want to wait for me. My horse will take some time to regain its strength."

"Allow me to carry the load," said Caleb.

All agreed that Caleb could handle the load without tiring, and the horse said it could proceed immediately without having to carry anything on its back.

After they rested for a while – how long exactly Caleb wasn't sure – they decided it was time to move on. They hoisted the packs onto Caleb's hump, put out the campfire, and proceeded toward the bright star in the sky.

The wind sang its secret songs, and voices floated on the air – a faint breath of words and music. The star had stopped running ahead of them, and they were coming closer to it. Soon, it would be directly overhead. They approached the outskirts of a town, the desert transforming into rocky hills and olive trees. The temperature dropped and the arid heat fell behind.

Shepherds and animals appeared, moving toward the town. The place was known as the City of David, and an inn stood on the periphery, on the route into the center.

"We are here," said Caspar.

As they approached, they could see a fire

burning in a barn. Some people were gathered around the entry. They heard a baby crying. They entered to see a man, a woman, and child.

Caspar approached and laid out frankincense as a gift.

Mel stepped forward and offered the fragrant myrrh.

And finally, Zar removed the packs from Caleb's back and laid the gold upon the hay in front of the baby.

Caleb stepped forward and found a spot upon which to lay and behold the child that was named Jesus.

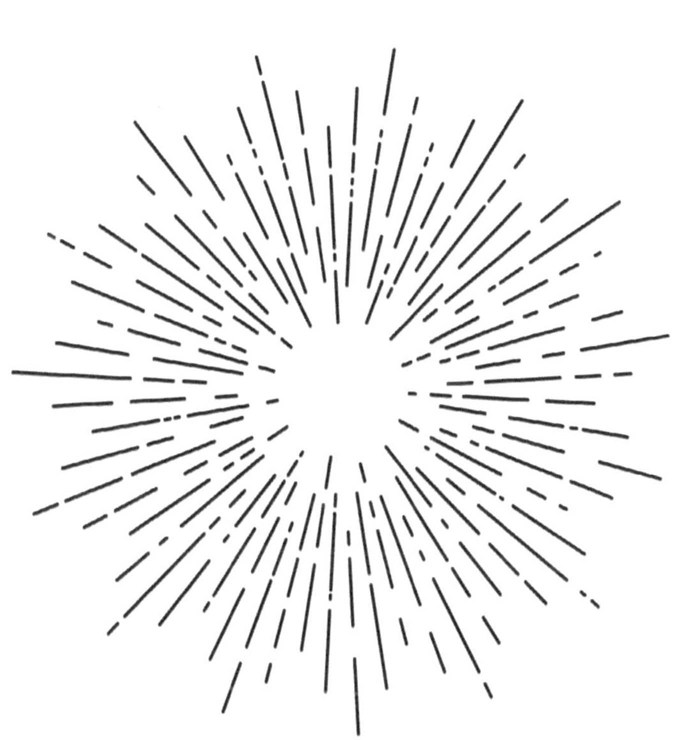

When the two men in green uniforms hoisted the tree into the hopper, Jake lowered his head and tears burned in the corner of his eyes.

Caleb was gone forever.

He ran to his room, threw himself onto the bed, and buried his tears in the blanket. Before long, he dozed off. When he awoke, he rolled over and stared at the ceiling. He didn't know how much time had passed, but the light outside was fading. He thought about Miss Bishop and how disappointed she would be that Caleb was gone. Jake had laid him on one of the tree branches and thought his mother had put Caleb back in place in front of the manger.

Jake had labored to sand Caleb's coat and to chisel his face and legs just so. His first woodshop project had been Noah's Ark. Miss Bishop had taught him how to rough out the basic shapes and then whittle and chisel to begin detailing each individual animal. She showed him how to sand and smooth, and then go back and chisel if needed, creating a continuous process until the object of his creation was to his liking. It was arduous but satisfying.

Jake worked hard, and Miss Bishop gave him ample attention and guidance because of his interest and devotion to his projects. Jake always talked about making everything perfect, but Miss Bishop cautioned that nothing and no-one is perfect. We all have some flaws somewhere, but that doesn't make us any less special, she said. She encouraged him to pour his love and affection into his work. That was the role of the creator.

Noah's Ark sat on top of Jake's bookshelf next to the Nativity, which was his second project. Jake loved the stories from the Bible, so it was easy for him to come up with ideas for his class projects. The giraffes had been his favorite animals in Noah's Ark, and the camel had been his favorite in the Nativity. Jake felt that the animals in this story didn't get enough attention, particularly the one with the hump on his back. Jake whispered to Caleb as he sanded his coat. Jake told Caleb how important he was to the story and how the future – Caleb's future, and Jake's future – depended on this story.

Jake sighed, rolled on his side, and looked up at the Nativity.

He was there!

Caleb was there, settled in front of the manger, in the place he was meant to be.

"Mom, Mom!" Jake ran out of the room.

Afterword

Caleb came to life in the early 2000s. After the new year, Tom and I would put away the Christmas decorations and place the tree on the curb to await the truck and its destiny. For several years just prior to having the glorious pine carted away, we would discover a stray ornament accidentally left on the tree and marvel at our oversight. One night, very late, Tom and I were in bed talking about the day and the almost lost ornament. I shared that a story had come to me, and I told him an early version of the tale you have just read. Tom loved the idea, and he reached over and pulled off the blankets and told me to go to my desk and write it down lest I forget it as could happen with a dream. So, I rose, made a cup of tea, and went to my desk in the wee hours to capture Caleb and his story.

Acknowledgments

I'd like to begin by thanking my critical readers: Tom Glymph, Linda Greigg, Jayne Marshall, Brenda Page, and Claire Wirdnam. A heartfelt thank you for your encouragement, specific ideas about the story, edits, and your love of Caleb.

A tremendous debt of gratitude to my friend and editor Jayne Marshall. I appreciate the valuable insights about story, perspectives, and language. And for being such a Caleb fan!

Most especially, I thank my beloved Tom — for the encouragement to capture Caleb when he came and for the years of love and support.

And a special shout out to my buddy Caleb and for the wonderful time we've been together, though I'm not sure how long that has been...

About the Author

Maria Glymph is a versatile writer on a lifelong creative journey. After a successful business career, she transitioned to a literary path, founded Modern Odyssey Books, and produced her debut poetry collection, *Barn Quilt*. In early 2024, Maria developed and began publishing the *In Search of…* puzzle book series, designed to make timeless literature both accessible and engaging for contemporary audiences.

She is currently working on a novella, expanding her poetry repertoire, and curating two anthologies to showcase the work of fellow writers.

Keep up with her at www.mariaglymph.com.

Modern Odyssey Books

Modern Odyssey Books publishes literary fiction, poetry, creative nonfiction, short story collections, and literature-inspired puzzle books.

We take readers on the magical and adventurous journey of words and stories.

Our books are available across all Amazon marketplaces, and we partner with Ingram Spark for international distribution.

www.modernodysseybooks.com

A collection of
poems by Maria
Glymph

Barn Quilt is the
tender expression of
friendship, grief, and
loss set in the North
Carolina farmland.

Go **In Search of Charles Dickens** and discover his famous novels, vivid characters, and his trademark wit.

Considered one of the greatest novelists of the Victorian era, Dickens penned many enduring stories, including *Oliver Twist*, *Great Expectations*, *David Copperfield*, *A Tale of Two Cities*, and *A Christmas Carol*.

Solve the puzzles while exploring the people and plots of his novels. Chuckle at his humor, and admire his cleverness.

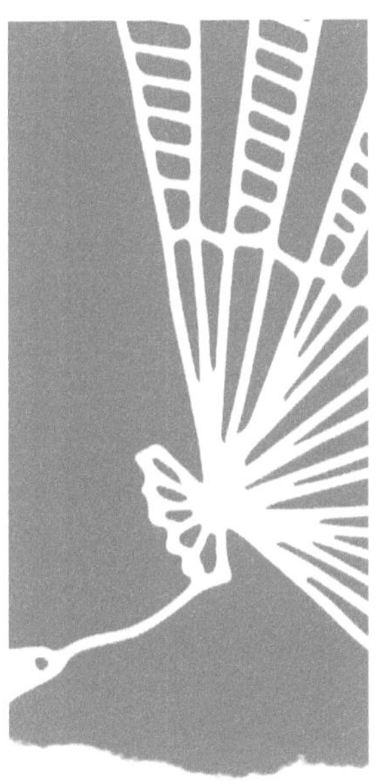

Go *In Search of Jane Austen* and discover her famous novels, characters who fall in love, and her keen observations about people and relationships. Austen's beloved novels of manners and romance include *Sense and Sensibility*, *Pride and Prejudice*, *Emma*, and *Persuasion*.

Solve the puzzles while exploring the people and plots of her novels, her literary lexicon, and the letters she often penned. In addition, there are a few surprises to relish.

Go ***In Search of the Brontë Sisters*** and discover their literary treasures. The three siblings initially wrote under pseudonyms and later became famous for their enduring contributions to literature – *Jane Eyre*, *Wuthering Heights*, and *The Tenant of Wildfell Hall*.

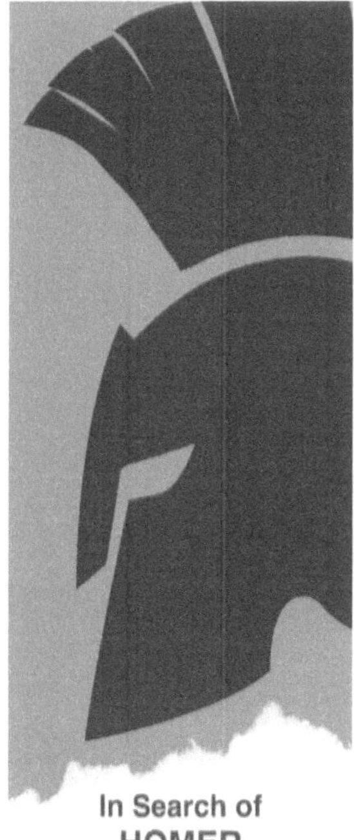

Go *In Search of Homer* and discover the Trojan War, the wrath of Achilles, and the journey of Odysseus. The blind poet is credited with two masterpieces – *The Iliad* and *The Odyssey* – and these timeless epic narratives set the course for unexpected puzzle fun.

MODERN
ODYSSEY